12,000 Miles From Home

by
Malachy Doyle

Illustrations by Greg Gormley

FRANKLIN WATTS
NEW YORK • LONDON • SYDNEY

1

London, 1950

"Jack, Jack, Mother Penguin wants to see us!"

Lucy Browning ran across the yard, crashing into her twin brother just as he was about to save a goal.

"Oh, look what you made me do,

silly!" cried Jack, as the football flew
past him.

"What does she want now, anyway?"
he muttered, as they walked down the long

corridor to the office. Inside they found a tall man, standing next to the nun who ran the children's home, the one they called Mother Penguin because of the long black dress she always wore.

"Ah, the twins!" said the nun, smiling.
"Sit down, both of you, and listen to
Mr. Carstairs."

"Hello, children," said the man, "I've

come to ask you a big question. How would you like to go to Australia?"

There was a long silence.

"Isn't that where kangaroos come from?" asked Lucy. She'd seen one in London Zoo.

The man laughed. "That's right, Lucy. The land of kangaroos, on the other side of the world, where the sun shines every day and the children ride to school on horseback."

"But why do you want to send us away, Mother Peng..., I mean Mother Superior?" asked Jack. "What have we done wrong?"

"You've done nothing wrong, Jack,"

the nun answered. "In fact, it's because you're such good children that Mr. Carstairs is giving you this chance."

Jack didn't believe her. He was always getting into trouble of one sort or another.

"Where would we live?" asked Lucy.

"Oh, there are lots of families out there looking to take in fine healthy-looking youngsters like you," the man replied. "You'll have pocket money every week, and when you grow up you'll be able to choose any job you like."

"But we don't want to live with strangers half way across the world!" said

Jack. "This is our home. And anyway Mum's coming back for us soon, isn't she, Lucy?"

Jack looked at Lucy. Lucy looked at Mother Superior.

"I'm very sorry, children," said the old nun, "but you won't be seeing your mother again."

"What do you mean?" asked Lucy, frightened.

"Oh dear," said the nun. "I knew we should have told you before, but I didn't want to upset you. Your Mum's been very ill, and a few weeks ago she passed away."

It was a very special ring. There were three gold bands that fitted together, and when their mother had brought Jack and Lucy to the children's home she'd given each twin one of the bands.

"Keep them safe, children," she'd told them, "and I'll keep the third one. As soon as I find a job and somewhere for us to live I'll come back for you. Then the ring will be complete and we'll be a family again."

Jack tried to fit the two pieces together,

but it didn't work without the third.

"I don't believe Mum's dead," he said. "It's a lie!"

"Why would they lie to us, Jack?" said Lucy, quietly, "It doesn't make any sense."

"I don't know," said Jack, "But what about Australia, Lucy? Do you really want to live so far from home."

"The nuns are kind here, Jack," Lucy answered, "and I'll miss my friends, but it isn't home. A real home is where you're one of the family, where you're loved. If Mum's not coming back, and someone else will give us a real home together, then

I don't care where it is."

They talked for a long time and at last Jack agreed. So the next morning they told the Mother Superior that they'd go. They were taken to buy a new set of clothes, and a few days later it was time to leave. After saying goodbye to all their friends, they were taken to the station by one of the younger nuns, Sister Winifred, to catch the train for the port of Southampton.

Jack and Lucy took their seats in the front carriage and settled down for the journey. It was noisy up by the engine, so they didn't hear what happened next.

As the whistle blew and the train began to pull out of the station, a young woman ran onto the platform.

"Jack! Lucy! Where are you? Don't leave me!" she cried, running along beside the train.

Jack and Lucy's mother clung to a door handle, beating desperately on the window, but the train picked up speed and she

was unable to hold on. She watched helplessly as it pulled out of the station, taking her children away from her forever.

Sister Winifred came and helped the poor woman away.

"It's all for the best, Miss Browning," she said, soothingly. "It's all for the best."

3

S.S. Corona

"Goodbye, England," cried Lucy, as the ship pulled away from the quay. She and Jack were up on deck, with all the other child migrants, waving farewell.

For most of the children it was the most exciting day of their lives. They were

dressed in smart new clothes, they'd had a ride on a steam train and now they were on a great ocean-going liner, sailing out to sea.

A little boy tugged Lucy's skirt. He couldn't have been more than five.

"Hello," he said. "I'm Alfie. Are you going to kangaroo land too?"

"Yes," said Lucy,

smiling down at him. "Isn't it exciting?"

"I'm not sure," said the boy, frowning. "When do we come back?"

Lucy looked at the boy closely. "We're not coming back, I'm afraid. We're going there to live."

"But what about my Mummy?" said the boy, his eyes filling with tears. "My Mummy's in England."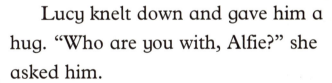

Lucy knelt down and gave him a hug. "Who are you with, Alfie?" she asked him.

"No one," said Alfie. "There's just me."

"Stay with me and my brother Jack then," said Lucy, smiling, " We'll

look after you."

There were hundreds of children on board, from all over England, Scotland, Wales and Ireland. They spent their time swapping stories about what life would be like in Australia, stories they'd been told

and stories they made up.

It was a long voyage, and many of the children were seasick, but it was a happy time for most of them. The crew and the other passengers were kind, and an air of excitement filled the ship.

4
Australia

"Welcome to Western Australia, children," said the Archbishop, six weeks and twelve thousand miles later. The ship had pulled into Fremantle harbour, and a band played 'Waltzing Matilda' as the boys and girls marched down the steps,

clutching their
suitcases and
blinking in the
bright sunshine.

"We're very short
of young white
people here," the
Archbishop continued,
"and that's why we've invited
you to our country. The boys will go with
the Christian Brothers, where you will be
educated and trained for farm work. The
girls will stay with the Sisters of Mercy and
learn all the skills you need to be farmers'
wives. You will become good Australians,
and we will be proud of you. God bless
you all."

"That's not right," said Jack to Digger,
a crew member he'd made friends with.
"What does he mean, we'll go with the

nuns and the Brothers? I thought they were going to find homes for us, homes with families!"

"So did I," said Digger. "That's what they told us on the boat. But it turns out it's not true. No one's going to families at all. The girls are going to a children's home in Perth, and you boys are all going to a new one out in the bush."

"You mean we'll be split up – me and Lucy?" said Jack, horrified.

"Looks like it," said Digger, sadly.

"Over my dead body!" said Jack. He ran to find Lucy and, above all the noise, explained to her what was about to happen.

Already the girls were being called over

to one side of the docks, where the nuns were waiting.

"We're going to have to escape, Lucy," said Jack. "Follow me."

They grabbed their suitcases and edged to the outside of the crowd. When they thought no one was looking they dashed away down the quay.

"Hey!" shouted a voice, "You two, come back!"

As a young Christian Brother gave chase, Jack and Lucy picked up speed.

They thought they were heading into town, but they hadn't gone far when they came to the end of the quay. In front of them was nothing but water.

Jack looked all around, desperately. He noticed a gap in the wall beside them.

"Quick, up here!" he shouted, pulling Lucy away.

They ran up the alleyway, but it turned out that was a dead end too. It lead to a high wall, which they were trying to climb when the Brother caught up with them.

"Got you!" he said, grabbing hold of them by the scruff of their necks.

"You can't split us up," shouted Jack, struggling to get away. "We're twins!"

"We can do what we want, boy," said

the Brother, gasping for breath. "It's the will of God."

"But they said we were going to a family," Jack shouted. "They said we'd stay together!"

"They were wrong," said the Brother, angrily. "Now stop wriggling and come with me."

With a final jerk, Jack managed to pull away from the man's grasp. He ran back down the alleyway, but it was too late. Four more Christian Brothers came round the corner, blocking any chance of escape. They were caught.

5
Bindoon

"I'll be keeping my eye on you, Jack Browning," said Brother Alban, pushing Jack onto the bus that was to take the boys to their new home. "We don't like trouble-makers at Bindoon."

The open-topped bus drove through

the city and out into the dusty countryside.
It wasn't green like England, it was brown
and dry. The hot sun burnt down on Jack,
Alfie and the others, hurting their eyes.

At last they arrived at Bindoon, but
instead of a children's home all they saw
were fields, trees, rubble and rock. They
were led into a hut where their new suits,
the ones they were so proud of, were taken
away. So were their shoes and socks, all
the other clothes they'd been given, and

even their suitcases. All they had to wear was a vest each and a pair of old baggy shorts. No shoes, no underwear, nothing.

★★★

The next morning they were made to get up at six thirty. Breakfast was a small glass of milk and a hunk of stale bread, and then they were sent outside in their bare feet to help build the children's home they were to live in.

Some had to clear stones from the fields, dragging them by rope to the building site. Others had to spend all day, from morning to night, mixing cement. By evening the boys were choking with the dust and badly burnt by the sun, as their bodies weren't used to the heat, and there was no shade. And by the time they got to bed, tired and hungry, they were wishing they'd never even heard of Australia.

★★★

This went on for a few days until, one morning at breakfast, Jack snapped.

"Why do you get eggs and bacon while we're given food that isn't fit for pigs!" he shouted at the Brothers. "And what about school? I thought you were supposed to be teaching us things, not just making us do all this work for you!"

Brother Alban hurried over and pushed Jack back into his seat.

"Be quiet, boy!" he hissed. "Hard work's all the education the likes of you will ever need. When it rains maybe we'll stay indoors and teach you to read and write, but while the sun shines you go out there and get on with it – unless you want to feel the weight of my strap on your backside!"

6

The Lost Ring

Lucy's new home wasn't much better.
Some of the nuns were kind, but others
were as cruel as the worst Christian
Brothers. Lucy's job was nearly as bad as
Jack's, for all day every day she had to
work in the laundry, washing and ironing.

It was hot and airless and she hated every moment. Lucy hid her band of the ring under her mattress. It was the only thing she had to remind her of her mother and Jack, to remind her that she was a real person, from a real family. Every night, after lights out, she took it out and traced its shape with her fingers.

★★★

One night Lucy reached under the thin mattress to find the ring, but it wasn't there. She felt all the way along the edge of the bed, but no, there was nothing.

She jumped out of bed and lifted up

the side of the mattress. Nothing. She felt
around on the floor. Nothing. She looked
around, desperately. In the half light she
saw Tracy Eakins, sitting up in the bed
opposite, grinning at her.

"What's wrong, Lucy? Lost something?"

"Have you taken it?" hissed Lucy,
furious. "Have you taken my ring?"

"That's for me to know and you to

find out," said Tracy, still grinning.

Lucy ran over to the other girl's bed and grabbed her by the hair. "Give it back!" she yelled. "Give it back now!"

Tracy screamed and grabbed a handful of Lucy's hair. Lucy cried out and a nun came running in.

"What's all this noise?" she cried. "Get back in bed right now, Lucy Browning! This is disgraceful behaviour!"

7
Mother Superior

The next morning Tracy and Lucy were called in to see the Mother Superior. No one dared to call this one Mother Penguin – she was a thin, old woman, with a face that never smiled. The girls were terrified of her, and some said she kept a leather strap in the drawer of her desk.

"Right, you two," she demanded, "I want to know what was going on last night, and I want to know NOW!"

"She stole my ring!" said Lucy, pointing at Tracy. "My mother's ring!"

"Is this true, Tracy?" asked the old nun.

"I did take it, Sister," said Tracy, shaking. "But I wasn't going to keep it. It's a stupid ring, anyway," she said, staring at Lucy. "It's all bent."

"Where's the ring now?" asked Mother Superior.

"Here, Sister," said Tracy, fetching it from her pocket, and handing it over.

The old woman opened the top drawer of her desk and dropped the ring in.

"I shall keep it in here, Lucy Browning. That way there'll be no more midnight squabbles."

"But Miss...,"

"Don't 'But Miss' me, young lady!" said the nun, taking a pair of scissors from the drawer. "Now come over here!"

Slowly Lucy approached the desk.

"Pulling each other's hair and behaving like animals!" said the nun. "Outrageous behaviour for young ladies. People may act like that in England, but it is not acceptable here in Australia, and I shall put a stop to it once and for all!"

She lifted a lock of Lucy's hair and hacked at it with the blunt scissors.

"No!" cried Lucy, trying to pull away, but the nun was gripping her tightly and pain ran through her.

"Stand still, girl!" shouted the nun, "Or I shall cut right into your head!"

Lucy stood there weeping, as her beautiful hair fell to the floor around her.

"Now you, Tracy!" demanded the nun, and Lucy had to stand and watch while the same happened to the other girl.

"Let that be a lesson to you both. Now get out of my sight, you ungrateful little hussies. No wonder your mothers didn't want you!"

8

On the Run

Lucy knew she had to leave. She waited until everyone else was asleep, and then she dressed, as quietly as possible, and crept down the back stairs to the Mother Superior's office. The door was locked, but when she went outside to try the window, she

found that it was slightly open.

She pushed it up, climbed in, and edged her way across the room in the darkness. She didn't dare turn on the light in case anyone saw, but in the darkness Lucy tripped over a chair, crashed into the desk and fell to the floor.

She gasped in horror – surely someone must have heard her! She crawled in under the desk and prayed that no one would come.

After what seemed like an age, Lucy decided it was safe. She stood up, felt for the drawer of the desk, and rummaged about inside until she found the ring.

Lucy was about to go when she

remembered the scissors. As she picked them up her fingers rubbed against the leather strap – the one that the old nun threatened to beat the girls with. Shuddering, she took it with her and climbed back out of the window.

Lucy ran down the street until she came to the river. She tossed the strap and the scissors high into the air. They each landed with a splash in the water, and Lucy punched the air in delight.

★★★

Lucy spent the night curled up in a shop doorway, shivering. She didn't sleep a wink, thinking of Jack. She knew he was in Bindoon, but how was she to get there? Then she remembered that once a week a truck arrived at her laundry, bringing the Christian Brothers' dirty washing.

The last place Lucy wanted to go was back to the nuns, but it was the only way to find Jack, so she had no choice. The delivery from Bindoon was due that morning, so Lucy crept back to the children's home before anyone was up. She hid in an empty laundry basket and waited until it was loaded onto the truck and driven off into the bush.

It was a hot and dusty ride, but at least Lucy knew that she was going to find her brother at last.

★★★

When they arrived at Bindoon, Lucy climbed out of the basket and hid, until a boy came to unpack the baskets.

It was little Alfie. He got the shock of his life when Lucy came out from her hiding place.

"Lucy!" he cried, throwing his arms round her. "What are you doing here?"

"Oh, Alfie," said Lucy, hugging him tightly, "How are you?"

"I don't like it, Lucy," he said, crying. "The Brothers are horrid to me. Please take me away."

Lucy knew then that she couldn't leave without Alfie. She told him her plan and asked him to go and fetch Jack.

★★★

At first Jack couldn't believe it was her.

"How did you find me, Lucy?" he said. "And what have they done to your hair?"

"I'll tell you later," said Lucy. "There's no time to talk now. Get your ring – we're leaving!"

Jack ran to fetch his band of their mother's ring and when he came back all three of them hid in the empty baskets that some older boys were loading onto the truck. The baskets were being taken to another children's home, even further out in the bush.

***

Jack felt like cheering as the truck went through the gates of Bindoon. When they'd gone a few miles the driver stopped for a smoke. Jack, Lucy and Alfie climbed out of the baskets, down from the back of the truck, and ran to a clump of trees. The man didn't notice, and drove off.

"We're free!" said Alfie, beaming.

"Yeah, we're free all right," said Jack. "But what do we do now? We've no money, nowhere to go, and I'm hungry already!"

9

The Bush

They started walking along the road. The
bush was empty, hot and dusty. After
about twenty minutes they saw a trail of
dust in the distance.

"It's a truck," said Jack. "Hide! They'll
send us back!"

Three times they did this, until Lucy
decided it didn't make any sense.

"We've got to take the risk," she said,
when the next one appeared. "It's our
only chance."

Though Jack was angry with her, Lucy
stood by the side of the road, in full view
of the truck. As it came near she put out
her hand. The driver slowed down, gave

her a long, hard look, but didn't stop.
Jack was furious. "He'll tell the Brothers!
They'll come and get us!"

Another truck appeared. Jack tried to
drag Lucy off the road, but she wouldn't
budge, so he ran to hide. The truck slowed
down, and this time it stopped.

An old farmer leaned out of the
window. "It's a hot day to be out

walking," he said, with a smile. "Hop in, girl, and I'll take you down the road a piece."

He was surprised to see another two children appear from behind a rock.

"So what on earth are you three doing out here in the middle of nowhere?" the driver asked, as they bounced along the dusty track. Lucy explained what had happened, and when she'd finished the man grinned.

"Well done, girl!" he said. "Me and Mabel, that's my wife, we're always saying it's a crying shame how you lot are

treated. I look after my sheep better!"

"You poor children," said Mabel,
when they arrived at the farmhouse.
"You look exhausted. Don't say a word till
you've had a bath, a hot meal, and a
good night's sleep."

★★★

The next morning, over breakfast, Lucy
explained what had happened and asked
Mabel if they could stay.

"Oh, I don't think so," said Mabel,
looking worried. "What would happen if

the Christian Brothers found out?"

But Tom wasn't frightened of anyone. "There's no way I'm going to let them go back," he said to Mabel. "Not after how they've been treated!"

He turned to the children. "You can stay here for a few days at least. Mabel and I will talk it over, and decide what to do."

9

A New Home

At last, one morning, Tom said, "Good news! We've decided we'd like to offer all three of you a place here with us. Isn't that right, Mabel?"

Mabel nodded.

"It feels like it's meant to be," she said,

with tears in her eyes. "You see, our two sons died in the war. We were heart-broken – I can't tell you what it's like to have no children, no grandchildren. So when we heard they were bringing orphans over from England, we asked if we could adopt one, or maybe two. They wouldn't let us – they said you had to stay with the nuns and the Brothers."

"There's no sign of anyone looking for you," said Tom. "I guess they're too worried about people finding out how badly they treated you. You'll be safe with us. If anyone asks, we'll tell them you're our nephews and niece over from England."

★★★

One evening after supper Jack and Lucy brought out their rings and told Tom and Mabel the whole story.

"They said Mum was dead, but it's not true," said Jack. "She's still looking for us, I know she is. I bet they said we're out here in the land of sunshine, riding to school on kangaroos. I bet they told her a pack of lies, just like they told us. But one day we'll find her, won't we, Lucy?"

Lucy nodded.

"What about me?" said Alfie, quietly. "What about my Mum?"

"We'll do everything we can to help you, Alfie," said Mabel. "It's a terrible thing they did to you poor children and

we'll try to put it right, at least for you three. Meanwhile you've a home here with us, a real home."

Lucy looked at Jack. "Can you remember talking about that back in England, Jack? About what it would be like to have a real home, together."

Jack nodded. "Of course I can, Lucy. You said a real home is where you're one of the family, where you're loved." He smiled across the table at Tom and Mabel. "This'll do for now."

Child Migration

The practice of sending British children to live thousands of miles away, without seeking the permission of their families, began in the early 19th century but continued right up until 1967.

The children were victims of poverty and broken homes and had been placed in orphanages and children's homes. It was believed that sending them abroad would give them a better chance in life, as well as saving money. As many as 150,000 children were shipped out to distant parts of the British Empire – Canada, Australia, New Zealand and Rhodesia (now Zimbabwe). Many of the children were told that they were orphans – that their parents and relatives had died, and so grew up unaware of their true identity. Their parents too were deceived – very few were made aware of what was to happen to their children.

Australia

The authorities were worried about the decline in population in Western Australia after the Second World War (1939–45). They were desperate to get

more white people to settle there, fearing that Asians would pour in from neighbouring countries and destroy their culture.

Around 8,000 children, mostly aged between seven and ten but some as young as three, were sent to Australia in this period, often being told only that they were going on holiday. Sadly the new life they were offered rarely lived up to the promises. The children were kept in large-scale institutions run by charities or religious orders. They were unloved, often poorly cared for, and in many cases treated with appalling cruelty.

Bindoon

Many child migrants were forced to do heavy manual labour. The boys at the

Bindoon Boys Camp near Perth, for example, which was run by Roman Catholic monks called Christian Brothers, had very little schooling. Instead they were made to clear stones from fields, mix cement, and basically build the home in which they lived.

The Child Migrants Trust

Great secrecy surrounded the child migration policies until, in 1986, a Nottingham social worker called Margaret Humphreys heard of a woman who said that she had been put on a boat to Australia at the age of four, cutting her off completely from her past, her identity and even her real name. At first Margaret found this hard to believe, but slowly she discovered that not only was the story true but that many thousands of young children had been treated in the same way. Margaret was horrified, and it became her mission to reunite as many child migrants as possible with their families before it was too late – before their parents died. Margaret went on to found the Child Migrants Trust and help thousands of people rediscover their roots.

Sparks: Historical Adventures

ANCIENT GREECE
The Great Horse of Troy – The Trojan War
0 7496 3369 7 (hbk)   0 7496 3538 X (pbk)
The Winner's Wreath – Ancient Greek Olympics
0 7496 3368 9 (hbk)   0 7496 3555 X (pbk)

INVADERS AND SETTLERS
Boudicca Strikes Back – The Romans in Britain
0 7496 3366 2 (hbk)   0 7496 3546 0 (pbk)
Viking Raiders – A Norse Attack
0 7496 3089 2 (hbk)   0 7496 3457 X (pbk)
Erik's New Home – A Viking Town
0 7496 3367 0 (hbk)   0 7496 3552 5 (pbk)

TALES OF THE ROWDY ROMANS
The Great Necklace Hunt
0 7496 2221 0 (hbk)   0 7496 2628 3 (pbk)
The Lost Legionary
0 7496 2222 9 (hbk)   0 7496 2629 1 (pbk)
The Guard Dog Geese
0 7496 2331 4 (hbk)   0 7496 2630 5 (pbk)
A Runaway Donkey
0 7496 2332 2 (hbk)   0 7496 2631 3 (pbk)

TUDORS AND STUARTS
Captain Drake's Orders – The Armada
0 7496 2556 2 (hbk)   0 7496 3121 X (pbk)
London's Burning – The Great Fire of London
0 7496 2557 0 (hbk)   0 7496 3122 8 (pbk)
Mystery at the Globe – Shakespeare's Theatre
0 7496 3096 5 (hbk)   0 7496 3449 9 (pbk)
Plague! – A Tudor Epidemic
0 7496 3365 4 (hbk)   0 7496 3556 8 (pbk)
Stranger in the Glen – Rob Roy
0 7496 2586 4 (hbk)   0 7496 3123 6 (pbk)
A Dream of Danger – The Massacre of Glencoe
0 7496 2587 2 (hbk)   0 7496 3124 4 (pbk)
A Queen's Promise – Mary Queen of Scots
0 7496 2589 9 (hbk)   0 7496 3125 2 (pbk)
Over the Sea to Skye – Bonnie Prince Charlie
0 7496 2588 0 (hbk)   0 7496 3126 0 (pbk)

TALES OF A TUDOR TEARAWAY
A Pig Called Henry
0 7496 2204 4 (hbk)   0 7496 2625 9 (pbk)
A Horse Called Deathblow
0 7496 2205 9 (hbk)   0 7496 2624 0 (pbk)
Dancing for Captain Drake
0 7496 2234 2 (hbk)   0 7496 2626 7 (pbk)
Birthdays are a Serious Business
0 7496 2235 0 (hbk)   0 7496 2627 5 (pbk)

VICTORIAN ERA
The Runaway Slave – The British Slave Trade
0 7496 3093 0 (hbk)   0 7496 3456 1 (pbk)
The Sewer Sleuth – Victorian Cholera
0 7496 2590 2 (hbk)   0 7496 3128 7 (pbk)
Convict! – Criminals Sent to Australia
0 7496 2591 0 (hbk)   0 7496 3129 5 (pbk)
An Indian Adventure – Victorian India
0 7496 3090 6 (hbk)   0 7496 3451 0 (pbk)
Farewell to Ireland – Emigration to America
0 7496 3094 9 (hbk)   0 7496 3448 0 (pbk)

The Great Hunger – Famine in Ireland
0 7496 3095 7 (hbk)   0 7496 3447 2 (pbk)
Fire Down the Pit – A Welsh Mining Disaster
0 7496 3091 4 (hbk)   0 7496 3450 2 (pbk)
Tunnel Rescue – The Great Western Railway
0 7496 3353 0 (hbk)   0 7496 3537 1 (pbk)
Kidnap on the Canal – Victorian Waterways
0 7496 3352 2 (hbk)   0 7496 3540 1 (pbk)
Dr. Barnardo's Boys – Victorian Charity
0 7496 3358 1 (hbk)   0 7496 3541 X (pbk)
The Iron Ship – Brunel's Great Britain
0 7496 3355 7 (hbk)   0 7496 3543 6 (pbk)
Bodies for Sale – Victorian Tomb-Robbers
0 7496 3364 6 (hbk)   0 7496 3539 8 (pbk)
Penny Post Boy – The Victorian Postal Service
0 7496 3362 X (hbk)   0 7496 3544 4 (pbk)
The Canal Diggers – The Manchester Ship Canal
0 7496 3356 5 (hbk)   0 7496 3545 2 (pbk)
The Tay Bridge Tragedy – A Victorian Disaster
0 7496 3354 9 (hbk)   0 7496 3547 9 (pbk)
Stop, Thief! – The Victorian Police
0 7496 3359 X (hbk)   0 7496 3548 7 (pbk)
A School – for Girls! – Victorian Schools
0 7496 3360 3 (hbk)   0 7496 3549 5 (pbk)
Chimney Charlie – Victorian Chimney Sweeps
0 7496 3351 4 (hbk)   0 7496 3551 7 (pbk)
Down the Drain – Victorian Sewers
0 7496 3357 3 (hbk)   0 7496 3550 9 (pbk)
The Ideal Home – A Victorian New Town
0 7496 3361 1 (hbk)   0 7496 3553 3 (pbk)
Stage Struck – Victorian Music Hall
0 7496 3363 8 (hbk)   0 7496 3554 1 (pbk)

TRAVELS OF A YOUNG VICTORIAN
The Golden Key
0 7496 2360 8 (hbk)   0 7496 2632 1 (pbk)
Poppy's Big Push
0 7496 2361 6 (hbk)   0 7496 2633 X (pbk)
Poppy's Secret
0 7496 2374 8 (hbk)   0 7496 2634 8 (pbk)
The Lost Treasure
0 7496 2375 6 (hbk)   0 7496 2635 6 (pbk)

20th-CENTURY HISTORY
Fight for the Vote – The Suffragettes
0 7496 3092 2 (hbk)   0 7496 3452 9 (pbk)
The Road to London – The Jarrow March
0 7496 2609 7 (hbk)   0 7496 3132 5 (pbk)
The Sandbag Secret – The Blitz
0 7496 2608 9 (hbk)   0 7496 3133 3 (pbk)
Sid's War – Evacuation
0 7496 3209 7 (hbk)   0 7496 3445 6 (pbk)
D-Day! – Wartime Adventure
0 7496 3208 9 (hbk)   0 7496 3446 4 (pbk)
The Prisoner – A Prisoner of War
0 7496 3212 7 (hbk)   0 7496 3455 3 (pbk)
Escape from Germany – Wartime Refugees
0 7496 3211 9 (hbk)   0 7496 3454 5 (pbk)
Flying Bombs – Wartime Bomb Disposal
0 7496 3210 0 (hbk)   0 7496 3453 7 (pbk)
12,000 Miles From Home – Sent to Australia
0 7496 3370 0 (hbk)   0 7496 3542 8 (pbk)